SAMURAI ASSASSIN

First published in Great Britain by HarperCollins *Children's Books* in 2014
HarperCollins *Children's Books* is a division of HarperCollins*Publishers* Ltd,
77-85 Fulham Palace Road, Hammersmith, London, W6 8JB.

The HarperCollins website address is: www.harpercollins.co.uk

1

Text © Hothouse Fiction Limited 2014
Illustrations © HarperCollins *Children's Books*, 2014
Illustrations by Dynamo

ISBN 978-0-00-794090-5

Printed and bound in England by Clays Ltd, St Ives plc

MIX
Paper from
responsible sources
FSC® C007454

FSC™ is a non-profit international organisation established to promote
the responsible management of the world's forests. Products carrying the
FSC label are independently certified to assure consumers that they come
from forests that are managed to meet the social, economic and
ecological needs of present and future generations,
and other controlled sources.

Find out more about HarperCollins and the environment at
www.harpercollins.co.uk/green

CHRIS BLAKE

TiME HUNTERS

SAMURAI ASSASSIN

HarperCollins *Children's Books*

Travel through time with Tom
on more

adventures!

Gladiator Clash

Knight Quest

Viking Raiders

Greek Warriors

Pirate Mutiny

Egyptian Curse

Cowboy Showdown

Samurai Assassin

Outback Outlaw

Stone Age Rampage

Mohican Brave

Aztec Attack

CONTENTS

With special thanks to Martin Howard

PROLOGUE

1500 AD, Mexico

As far as Zuma was concerned, there were only two good things about being a human sacrifice. One was the lovely black pendant the tribal elders had given her to wear. The other was the little Chihuahua dog the high priest had just placed next to her.

I've always wanted a pet, thought Zuma, as the trembling pup snuggled up close. *Though this does seem like an extreme way to get one.*

Zuma lay on an altar at the top of the Great Pyramid. In honour of the mighty Aztec rain god, Tlaloc, she'd been painted bright blue and wore a feathered headdress.

The entire village had turned out to watch the slave girl be sacrificed in exchange for plentiful rainfall and a good harvest. She could see her master strutting in the crowd below, proud to have supplied the slave for today's sacrifice. He looked a little relieved too. And Zuma couldn't blame him. As slaves went, she was a troublesome one, always trying to run away. But she couldn't help it – her greatest dream was to be free!

Zuma had spent the entire ten years of her life in slavery, and she was sick of it. She knew she should be honoured to be a sacrifice, but she had a much better plan – to escape!

"Besides," she said, frowning at her painted skin, "blue is not my colour!"

"Hush, slave!" said the high priest, Acalan, his face hidden by a jade mask. "The ceremony is about to begin." He raised his knife in the air.

"Shame I'll be missing it," said Zuma. "Tell Tlaloc I'd like to take a *rain* check." As the priest lowered the knife, she pulled up her knees and kicked him hard in the stomach with both feet.

"*Oof!*" The priest doubled over, clutching his belly. The blade clattered to the floor.

Zuma rolled off the altar, dodging the other priests, who fell over each other in their attempts to catch her. One priest jumped into her path, but the little Chihuahua dog sank his teeth into the man's ankle. As the priest howled in pain, Zuma whistled to the dog.

"Nice work, doggie!" she said. "I'm getting

out of here and you're coming with me!" She scooped him up and dashed down the steps of the pyramid.

"Grab her!" groaned the high priest from above.

Many hands reached out to catch the slave girl, but Zuma was fast and determined. She bolted towards the jungle bordering the pyramid. Charging into the cool green leaves, she ran until she could no longer hear the shouts of the crowd.

"We did it," she said to the dog. "We're free!"

As she spoke, the sky erupted in a loud rumble of thunder, making the dog yelp. "Thunder's nothing to be scared of," said Zuma.

"Don't be so sure about that!" came a deep voice above her.

Zuma looked up to see a creature with blue skin and long, sharp fangs, like a jaguar. He carried a wooden drum and wore a feathered headdress, just like Zuma's.

She knew at once who it was. "Tlaloc!" she gasped.

The rain god's bulging eyes glared down at her. "You have dishonoured me!" he bellowed. "No sacrifice has ever escaped before!"

"Really? I'm the first?" Zuma beamed

with pride, but the feeling didn't last long. Tlaloc's scowl was too scary. "I'm sorry!" she said quietly. "I just wanted to be free."

"You will *never* be free!" Tlaloc hissed. "Unless you can escape again…"

Tlaloc banged his drum, and thunder rolled through the jungle.

He pounded the drum a second time, and thick black clouds gathered high above the treetops.

"This isn't looking good," Zuma whispered. Holding the dog tightly, she closed her eyes.

On the third deafening drum roll, the jungle floor began to shake and a powerful force tugged at Zuma. She felt her whole body being swallowed up inside… the drum!

CHAPTER 1
RAIN STOPS PLAY

Tom looked out of the window and grinned. It was a beautiful summer's day, and he couldn't wait to get outside.

"You're going to love tennis," he said to Zuma. "It's great fun."

Zuma picked up Tom's tennis racquet and looked at it curiously. A frown wrinkled her blue-painted face. "What's this?" she asked. "Is it some sort of weapon?" Without waiting for a reply, the Aztec girl shrieked a battle cry and took a wild swing with the racquet.

Tom yelped as she knocked one of his mum's best ornaments off a shelf. He dived across the room, catching the china figure just before it hit the floor.

"Be careful!" he gasped. "You know I'm the only person who can see and hear you. If you break anything, *I'll* get the blame!"

A low growl made Tom turn round. Chilli, Zuma's Chihuahua dog, was crouched on the sofa, baring his teeth at one of the cushions as though it was a rival dog. Then he leaped on the cushion and began pulling out the stuffing with his teeth.

Tom groaned. "And *please* keep Chilli under control," he added.

Zuma wasn't listening. She was still inspecting the tennis racquet. "It's not very sharp," she said. "Which part do you hit your enemies with?"

Tom grabbed the racquet out of Zuma's hands before she could do any more damage.

"It isn't a weapon. Tennis is a *game*," he explained. "Two players use these racquets to hit a ball to each other across a net."

"Oh, a *game*," Zuma replied. "My people had games too."

Tom instantly forgot about Chilli eating his mum's cushions. He loved history and hearing Zuma's stories about the Aztec world. "What sort of games?" he asked.

"The most popular was called Ulama," Zuma told him. "Two teams knocked a ball round a court using their hips. The ball was very heavy so the players were always covered in bruises. Though of course it didn't matter for some of them."

"Let me guess," said Tom. "The players were sacrificed after every game, right?"

"Don't be silly!" Zuma rolled her eyes. "Only the *losing* team was sacrificed."

Tom shook his head. He was amazed that Zuma could talk about human sacrifice so calmly. After all, she had narrowly escaped being sacrificed to the rain god, Tlaloc! Though the Aztec god did get his own back by magically trapping her in a drum. And if Tom hadn't beaten the drum in his dad's museum, she'd still be locked inside it.

Since then, Tom

had been trying to help Zuma win back her freedom by finding six gold coins that Tlaloc had scattered throughout time. They had found one in the American Wild West, but there were five more to collect – and Tom knew Tlaloc wasn't going to make their challenges easy!

But until the god appeared again, there was time for a game of tennis. And Zuma and Chilli could cause less damage in the garden than they could inside Tom's house.

"Come on," he said firmly. "There's another racquet in the shed. I'll show you how to play."

Opening the back door to the garden, Tom blinked in surprise. Seconds ago the sky had been bright and sunny. Now it was pouring with rain!

Zuma nervously peered outside. "Is it

Tlaloc?" she asked. The Aztec god usually appeared in a cloud of rain.

"I don't think so," replied Tom. "It's probably just a shower. But we can't play tennis now. Let's go inside and play on my computer instead."

He led the way upstairs, Chilli bounding round his ankles.

"Com-puter?" said Zuma. "What's that?"

But Tom didn't get a chance to explain. As he walked into his bedroom, he stopped suddenly, making Zuma walk into his back. Chilli began growling.

"Uh-oh!" said Tom quietly. It was raining *inside* his bedroom.

Tom and Zuma looked up. The ceiling was covered with dark, swirling clouds. Thunder rumbled and a loud, threatening laugh boomed out.

"Tlaloc!" cried Zuma.

The face of the Aztec god formed in the clouds above them. His skin was as blue as Zuma's. Eyes bulged out of his feathered head. When Tlaloc opened his mouth, Tom saw two rows of sharp fangs. He gulped. The god looked even angrier than before.

"Tremble, slave – it is indeed Tlaloc!" the god thundered. "Enough games! It is time for your next challenge. And this time you will not be so lucky…"

Before Tom could say anything, Tlaloc's face disappeared. The rain grew softer, turning into a sparkling mist. Chilli whimpered, and Zuma scooped up the little dog into her arms. As the mist thickened, Tom felt like he was standing on air. He closed his eyes as he travelled down the tunnels of time.

CHAPTER 2
FAR FROM HOME

And then, suddenly, Tom felt solid ground beneath his feet.

"Where are we?" Zuma asked.

Nervously, Tom opened his eyes. He never knew where they were going to end up next. This time they were standing on a grassy plain, surrounded by hills. There was no one else in sight. The only sounds were the breeze blowing through the knee-high grass and the chirping of crickets.

Tom shaded his eyes from the hot sun with his hands.

"I've no idea," he said. "All I can see is grass and hills. We could be anywhere."

"Well, you're the history expert," said Zuma. "What about these clothes – are they a clue?"

Tom turned and saw that the Aztec girl's blue body paint had vanished, revealing her glowing, golden-brown skin. Her feathered headdress had also disappeared and her dark hair was pulled into a tight topknot above her head. She was dressed in a long yellow robe with loose sleeves, tied in place by a wide white belt. Her shoes looked like wooden flip-flops.

"Well? Got any ideas?" she asked.

Tom looked down at himself. He was wearing a similar robe, though his was grey with a black belt. He nodded. "I've seen these clothes before, in books. They're called kimonos. The Japanese wear them. So we must be in Japan."

Zuma frowned.

"Japan is an island country in the Pacific Ocean," Tom told her. "We're a long way from home."

"Wherever we are, Tlaloc's gold coin is here somewhere," said Zuma. "You don't think it's hidden in all this grass, do you? We'll be here *forever*."

"And it would be the most boring quest ever," Tom added.

"It doesn't sound like Tlaloc's style, does it?" Zuma said. "He's much more of a 'horrible screaming danger' type of god."

"Why don't you ask your necklace?" Tom suggested. "It helped us before."

Zuma's necklace had a black pendant with special powers. Last time they had travelled through time, it had given them a riddle with clues to help them find the gold coin.

"Good idea," said Zuma. She grinned. "I knew there was a reason I let you come along."

Holding up the black pendant, Zuma chanted:

"Mirror, mirror, on a chain,
Can you help us? Please explain!
We are lost and must be told
How to find the coins of gold."

Tom waited, holding his breath. Slowly, silver letters began to emerge on the pendant's polished surface. They spelled out another riddle:

In the land of warriors, great and old,
A pinch of salt is worth its weight in gold.
The Tiger's claws will leave a scar;
What keeps you cool may take you far.
Act with honour to impress a lord;
Heroes not thieves will get their reward.
When all is dark make for the light
Beware the masked man who walks in the night.

The two of them stared at the letters in silence. Tom was the first to speak. "I don't understand," he said. "What's salt got to do with anything?"

Zuma flapped her hand to shush him. "Be quiet! I can hear something," she whispered.

Tom listened closely. Sure enough, there was a thunderous rumble in the distance. It sounded like it was getting closer.

"Oh no, not Tlaloc again," he groaned.

"It's not Tlaloc," said Zuma. "Look – over there!"

Tom's eyes followed Zuma's pointing finger. She had spotted a tall teenage boy sprinting down a hill as if his life depended on it.

A few seconds later, Tom saw why.

The noise wasn't thunder – it was the hooves of galloping horses. A group of

horsemen charged over the hill. Their leader
saw the running boy and pointed, screaming
at the men behind. He urged his sweating
horse to go faster. Looking over his shoulder,
the boy yelled in fright. The horsemen were
gaining on him. He put on a fresh spurt of
speed, heading straight for Tom and Zuma.

As the horsemen drew nearer, Tom
recognised their armour from an exhibit in
his dad's museum. It belonged to medieval
Japanese warriors called samurai. Each
warrior wore an iron breastplate, and skirts
of overlapping leather protected their legs.
Their helmets were decorated with what

looked like alien antennae. Strapped to the samurai's backs were curved swords called *katana*. In the safety of the museum, Tom had thought the *katana* looked really cool. Up close they looked like deadly weapons.

"They're samurai warriors!" he called out to Zuma.

"They're big bullies, that's what they are!" she shouted back.

The boy was only a few metres from Tom and Zuma when he stumbled, twisting his ankle. He fell to the ground with a cry of pain.

Before Tom could blink, Zuma had run over to his side. "Can you get up?" she asked. "Here… lean on me."

"Lean on me too," added Tom, running over to join them. Whatever magic Tlaloc used to transport them across time also

made it possible for Tom and Zuma to communicate with everyone they met.

"Don't worry about me," the boy panted, staggering to his feet. "Get out of here before they catch you as well!"

"Tom!" shouted Zuma.

When Tom looked up, his face went white with fear. A wave of samurai horsemen was crashing down on them!

CHAPTER 3
SALT THIEF

Tom's heart thumped like a drum. There was nowhere to hide. The tiny part of his brain that wasn't terrified told him it was useless to run. There was no way to escape the galloping horses. The three of them, and Chilli, would be trampled beneath the flying hooves.

He closed his eyes. Then a voice shouted, "Halt!"

Tom opened his eyes, amazed he was still

alive. The samurai had pulled up their horses at the last second, and were now fanning out round Tom, Zuma and the boy. Within seconds, they were surrounded.

The same voice that had given the command spoke again. "Who are *you*?" it said, in a sneering tone.

Tom looked up. The samurai leader was glaring down at him from the back of his snorting black stallion. Beneath all the heavy armour, Tom could see he was a young man – barely older than the boy he had been chasing. His face was proud, his eyes cruel and arrogant.

"We're travellers," Tom said quickly.

At his feet, Chilli growled. "Good doggie. Brave doggie," whispered Zuma, trying to calm down her pet.

"Well, *travellers*, I am Goro, the son of an

important nobleman. You may bow."

Zuma snorted loudly. "I don't think so," she said. "I don't bow to anyone."

Goro's eyes blazed with anger. "You try to help Oda, the salt thief, and then you refuse to bow?" he barked. "Do you wish to share his punishment?"

"Salt thief?" giggled Zuma. "He stole some *salt*? Is that all?"

"Be silent, girl!" Goro commanded.

Zuma ignored him. "What a mighty warrior you are," she taunted. "Leading your men in a brave quest to capture a salt thief."

Goro's face had turned purple with rage. Tom elbowed Zuma. "Have you seen their swords?" he whispered. "Maybe you shouldn't—"

"Enough!" screamed Goro. "Perhaps watching me thrash Oda until he is black and blue will silence you." He held up a thick bamboo cane and the sunlight flashed on a silver ring he wore on his finger.

"Don't you dare," snapped Zuma. She stamped her foot. "I used to be a slave, so I know what it's like to be unfairly punished. If you want to thrash him, you'll have to get past me first."

"And me," Tom said, stepping in front of Oda.

Surprised, Goro lowered the cane. A sly grin crept across his face. "No," he said finally. "A thrashing would be too kind a punishment. The Dragon himself will punish you for your insolence."

Oda turned pale. Tom wanted to tell him not to worry and that there were no such things as dragons, but he decided to keep quiet. Goro was angry enough already. Whatever the samurai had meant, Tom knew that they had to escape. The riddle had mentioned a tiger, but said nothing about dragons. The last thing he wanted was to become a prisoner of the samurai.

It seemed Zuma had been thinking the same thing. "Look!" she cried out, pointing behind Goro. "Salt thief! And he's getting away!"

Goro grunted with surprise, and turned round in his saddle.

"Run!" Zuma hissed at Tom.

They both darted off in different directions, trying to find a gap in the ring of horsemen.

Tom managed to take two steps before he felt the sharp tip of a sword pressing into his chest. He stopped in his tracks. The samurai holding the sword smirked at him triumphantly. Looking across at Zuma, Tom saw that she had met the same fate. They were trapped.

"Nice try," said Goro. "But you're going nowhere."

Tom and Zuma could do nothing to stop one of the horsemen climbing down and tying their wrists together with rope, along with Oda's. Chilli buzzed round the Samurai's heels, yapping angrily.

"Tell your dog to be quiet," Goro said nastily. "Or he'll regret it."

"Shh, Chilli!" Zuma said. "Don't let that big meanie hurt you."

They began marching through the long grass, with samurai riders guarding them on either side. It wasn't easy keeping up with the horsemen. Tom and Zuma's feet were soon sore and the ropes dug painfully into their wrists. Marching was thirsty work. The sun was rising in the sky and it was getting hotter.

"Sorry for getting you into so much trouble," Oda whispered to Tom. "It was good of you to try and help me."

Tom looked up at the boy's anxious face. "Don't worry about it," he told him. "Zuma and I have been in tight spots before. But why were you stealing salt? I thought thieves liked gold and jewels."

"I'm no thief," Oda said stiffly. "The people in my village need salt to stop their food from rotting, so they can keep feeding themselves. But Goro has been keeping all the salt to himself. I was only stealing from him to stop my people from starving."

"What about this Dragon?" asked Zuma. "What's he got to do with all this?"

Oda looked at her as if she were mad. "You don't know who the Dragon is?" he said.

She shrugged. "Tom told you – we're travellers."

"Then you must be a *very* long way from home," said Oda. "Everyone knows Lord Uesugi Kenshin, the Dragon. He is the *daimyo* of Echigo Province."

"The what-yo?" Zuma blinked, shaking her head.

"A *daimyo* is a sort of powerful Japanese lord, isn't it?" Tom asked.

"Exactly," Oda replied. "Only the *shogun*, who rules the whole country, is more powerful than the Dragon."

"Is he as fierce as his name sounds?" Zuma asked.

"I have never seen him," Oda whispered, "but they say the Dragon is the most feared warrior in Japan, and a master of warfare."

Zuma wrinkled her nose at Tom. "I'm beginning to think that searching through the grass for my coin might have been more fun," she whispered.

"Too late for that," Tom told her, as they reached the top of a hill. "Look!"

Zuma gasped. Below them a city of tents stretched out across the valley, and smoke from the camp fires drifted across the sky. A thousand banners fluttered in the breeze. At the centre of the camp was a red tent that looked bigger than a mansion, ringed by guards. Two banners rose high into the air on either side of the entrance.

"Behold," Goro said triumphantly. "The Dragon's Lair!"

CHAPTER 4
THE DRAGON

Even though Tom was tired and thirsty after the long march across the plains, he still felt a thrill of excitement as they entered the samurai camp. The Dragon's men seemed to have only one thing on their minds – battle. The air rang with sharp cracks as warriors trained with wooden practice swords. Blacksmiths stood over blazing furnaces, sharpening weapons. Samurai warriors marched past in full armour, some wearing metal facemasks that were designed to look like demons. Others had helmets decorated with great wings or discs of metal.

Outside the Dragon's tent, Goro dismounted. Immediately, the guards stood aside for him. Goro's soldiers grabbed Tom, Zuma and Oda by their arms. The three prisoners were roughly pushed through the entrance of the tent.

It was dim inside. The air was thick with sweet-smelling smoke. In the centre a huge man with a long black moustache was sitting on a throne. He was wearing layers of thick black armour studded with bright red and blue beads. A pair of giant golden antlers rose from his helmet. Tom gulped. The man was the fiercest warrior he had ever seen. No wonder his nickname was the Dragon.

Servants scuttled out of the way as Goro

approached the throne. The Dragon said
nothing. His face was blank as he looked
down at the young samurai.

Goro bowed deeply. "My Lord Kenshin, I have brought criminals to face your justice." He held up a hand. A shove sent Tom stumbling forward. Zuma and Oda were also pushed in front of the throne.

"What is their crime?" The Dragon's voice was deep and rumbling.

Pointing at Oda, Goro said, "This one is a salt thief. These two travellers tried to help him escape. When I captured them, they spoke to me disrespectfully."

As Goro finished speaking, Oda sank to his knees. He bowed until his head was almost touching the floor. "Lord Dragon," he said, "I beg your forgiveness. I stole the salt because the people in my village are starving. Their food goes bad in the heat while the stores of Goro's castle are overflowing."

The Dragon's face darkened. His eyebrows

met in a scowl. Tom felt the blood drain from his face. Lord Kenshin looked furious.

Then, to Tom's amazement, the Dragon turned his angry face on Goro.

"Is this true?" he asked, his voice icy cold. "Do the people of your lands go hungry?"

"My Lord," said Goro. "They are only peasants. Who cares if—?"

The Dragon cut him off with a chop of his hand. "Your greed forces the innocent to starve while you have plenty," he bellowed. "You have no honour, and I will not have a man without honour in my army. Take your belongings and go back to your father's house."

Goro's jaw dropped open. "B-but my Lord," he stammered. "If I d-do not fight with you it w-will bring great shame on my family!"

"You have already brought great shame on your family!" the Dragon roared. "Now get out of my sight!"

For a moment it looked like Goro would argue. His mouth opened then closed again. Finally, shaking and pale, he bowed. Without another word, he turned and walked away in disgrace.

Tom had no time to enjoy the moment. The Dragon immediately turned back to the three prisoners. A servant came over and handed him a silver goblet brimming with water. At the sight of the goblet, Tom couldn't help licking his lips. He was really thirsty.

"You look like you need a drink, boy," said the Dragon. "Here."

Beckoning his servants forward, he told them to untie Tom, Zuma and Oda's hands.

Then the Dragon handed the goblet to Tom,
who took a large gulp of water. He passed
the goblet to Zuma, who did the same before
giving it to Oda.

"Water good?" asked the Dragon.

Tom nodded gratefully.

"Excellent," said the warlord, taking back the goblet. "Someone always taste the Dragon's water before he drinks. In case water poisoned."

Tom stared at him in disbelief. Suddenly the Dragon roared with laughter. He clapped Tom on the back so hard his teeth rattled.

"Don't worry – water not poisoned. The Dragon just likes to share a joke," he said. Now he was laughing he didn't seem nearly so fierce. He wiped a tear from his eye and drank the water in one swig. But when he had given the servant the empty goblet the Dragon's face was serious once more.

"Now, back to business," he said. He pointed at Oda. "Goro was wrong to hoard the salt," he told the boy. "But it is also wrong to steal."

Oda bowed again. "Yes, my Lord," he mumbled.

"I will give your village salt from my own stores," the Dragon continued. "But you will have to load every barrel on to the carts as punishment. And you will also spend a week working in my kitchens."

Oda looked happy, and relieved. Tom didn't think the teenager could bow any lower, but somehow he managed it. "It would be an honour, my Lord," he said. "May I also ask that you pardon my friends?" He pointed at Tom and Zuma. "Unarmed, they stood against Goro and twelve of his men. They risked their lives to save mine."

The Dragon looked from Tom to Zuma with new interest.

"You acted bravely," he said.

"It was nothing," said Tom, blushing. "We just happened to be there."

"Your modesty matches your courage," the Dragon replied. "It will be rewarded. You will do me the service of carrying my personal banner into battle."

Oda gasped. Carrying a warlord's banner was a mark of great respect.

"Battle, my Lord?" Tom swallowed nervously.

The Dragon smiled. "Perhaps you have not heard. My army is about to fight the Tiger."

Tom shot an excited glance at Zuma. The riddle had mentioned something about a tiger. She looked back at him, her eyebrows raised. She was clearly thinking the same thing – Tom had no choice but to accept the Dragon's offer.

"I will carry your banner, Lord Dragon," Tom said. "But isn't this a very big army to fight one animal?"

The Dragon roared with laughter, slapping his knee. "I see you like a joke too," he chuckled. "As I am called the Dragon, so my greatest rival, Lord Takeda Shingen, is called the Tiger. We have been at war for many years, and our greatest battle is about to begin. By joining it, you will earn a place in history."

Tom bowed, saying, "Thank you, Lord Dragon. He then turned to Oda. "Would you like some help loading the barrels of salt?" Tom asked.

"When I was a slave, I often went hungry," said Zuma. "I'll lend a hand too."

Again the Dragon looked impressed. He nodded at Tom and Zuma. "You can help

Oda, but be ready to ride to war when the time comes. It is time to clip the Tiger's claws."

As they left the tent, Tom's heart was in his mouth. He was going into battle! The riddle had said nothing about war. Honour was one thing, but he had seen the ferocious weapons and fighting skills of the samurai up close. Staying alive would be their biggest challenge yet…

CHAPTER 5
RING MASTER

Tom and Zuma puffed and panted as they heaved a heavy barrel of salt on to a cart. "This quest is turning out to be hard work," said Zuma, blowing out her cheeks.

"You can say that again," Tom agreed. He wiped sweat from his eyes. "These barrels weigh a ton!"

The flap to the store tent opened and Oda appeared. The gangly teenager was rolling yet another barrel towards the cart. "Only another sixty-eight to go," he grinned.

Tom and Zuma groaned. As Chilli sniffed round one of the barrels, the little dog discovered a small hole in the wood. He dived at it happily. Before Zuma could stop him, the dog licked at the salt. A second later, he jumped away with a yelp.

Zuma laughed. "Serves you right, you greedy pup," she said.

Oda chuckled too. Looking from Tom to Zuma, he said, "You two look hot. Why don't you take a break? I can lift these on my own."

Before Tom could protest, Oda lifted one of the heavy barrels as if it was filled with feathers.

"Thanks, Oda," said Zuma. She sat in the shade of the cart and poured Chilli a bowl of water. "Will you have enough salt for your village now?"

"More than enough," Oda replied, picking up another barrel.

"It was amazing that the Dragon just gave it to you," said Tom.

"It's not the first time he's sent salt to starving villages," Oda replied. "He once did the same for the people of the Tiger's province."

Tom frowned. "I thought the Tiger was his enemy," he said.

"The Lord Dragon is an honourable man," explained Oda. "He once said that 'Wars are to be won with swords and spears, not rice and salt.'"

"What does that mean?" Zuma asked.

"It means that to attack when your enemy's people are starving would be dishonourable. The samurai follow the path of *Bushido*. The rules are strict. Any samurai would prefer death to dishonour. To the samurai, honour is everything. A dishonourable victory would be worse than a defeat." He paused and reached into his pocket. "And speaking of honour, I have a gift for you."

Tom and Zuma looked at the small leather pouch Oda was holding out.

"You don't need to give us anything," said Tom.

"It's only a little salt," Oda said. "Thanks to the Dragon's generosity, my village will have plenty for a long time. Please take it as a mark of my thanks and friendship."

Tom took the pouch. "Thank you, Oda," he said.

"Hey, you!" a voice called out. Tom and Oda turned to see a grey-haired samurai walking towards them. "You with the barrel," the man shouted.

"Oh no! What trouble are we in *now*?" muttered Zuma.

"I've been watching the way you lift those things," said the samurai, looking Oda up and down. "You've got strength in that skinny body of yours."

Oda looked confused, but bowed.

The samurai slapped him on the shoulder. "I have organised some wrestling to entertain us while we wait for the battle to begin. You look like you might enjoy a match. Am I right?"

Oda nodded excitedly.

Half an hour later, Tom and Zuma were standing at the front of a cheering crowd. A large circle had been made in the ground. In the middle of the circle, Oda was wrestling a much larger man. They were wearing just simple cloths round their middles, and both of them were covered in sweat. It was the third match Tom and Zuma had watched and the rules were simple. The winner was the first man to force his opponent out of the ring or to make him touch the ground with any part of the body except his feet.

"Go on, Oda, pull him down!" Zuma yelled.

"Throw him out of the ring!" Tom shouted.

"He'll never win," said the grey-haired samurai who had organised the match.

"Kashegi is the Echigo Province champion. It was unlucky for your friend that he was picked to fight him."

Oda's opponent was a heavy, battle-scarred warrior. He was older than Oda and had muscles like tree trunks. But Oda was faster and almost as strong. As Kashegi charged, Oda dodged and caught the warrior in an unexpected grip. The crowd cheered.

"Your friend fights well," said the grey-haired samurai. He sounded surprised and pleased.

But just then Kashegi found his footing. He shoved back, hard. Oda staggered and almost fell.

Next to Tom, the grey-haired samurai said, "Your friend put up a good fight, but Kashegi is stronger. He will finish it now."

"Don't bet on it!" said Tom.

Once again, speed came to Oda's rescue. When Kashegi threw himself across the ring to finish him off, Oda ducked. He slammed his shoulder into the great samurai's belly and grabbed him round the legs. Then Oda straightened up with a massive effort. Tom could see his muscles straining as he lifted the huge warrior.

Yelling with shock, Kashegi was flipped over Oda's back. He landed on his own back in the middle of the circle with a loud *thump*.

The crowd exploded with applause and

Tom and Zuma cheered for their new friend. The grey-haired samurai clapped loudly. "I've never seen anything like it," he shouted over the noise. "He could become a great champion."

Ten minutes later, Oda was still grinning, even as they headed back to the cart.

"You were brilliant!" Zuma told him, for the sixteenth time.

"Incredible," Tom agreed. "You fight really well. Have you ever thought of becoming a samurai?"

The smile on Oda's face faded. "I would love to be a samurai," he said. "But most of them are sons of noblemen, like Goro. There is no room in their ranks for peasant farmers like me."

"Ha," said Zuma, with a scowl. "It's like when I was a slave. All anyone thought I was good for was hard work and being sacrificed."

Glumly, Oda continued. "All I could hope to become is a ninja."

"A ninja?" said Tom. "Like a hired

assassin? Cool!"

Oda shook his head. "The ninja are sneaky killers and cunning spies," he said disapprovingly. "They will stop at nothing if they are paid enough and they don't care about honour. I'd rather spend the rest of my life as a farmer."

Before Tom could ask Oda any more questions, a great drum boomed out across the Dragon's camp. Horns blared and commands rang out. The samurai stopped whatever they were doing and scrambled for their weapons.

"What's happening?" Zuma asked, looking round.

A second later she got her answer. One of the Dragon's servants darted through the crowd. Stopping in front of Tom, he bowed and said, "Lord Kenshin sends you this message: the Tiger's army has reached the plains. A horse and his banner are waiting for you. We ride to war at once!"

CHAPTER 6

HEAT OF BATTLE

The two great armies lined up, facing each other across a grassy plain. Warriors gripped their spears in silence, waiting for the order to charge. Some were on foot, some on horseback. Each warrior had his own banner attached to his back. Everyone was tense and stony-faced.

Tom and Zuma sat on horseback on a hill looking out over the battlefield. They had been ordered to watch the battle alongside the Dragon. Tom was holding the Dragon's banner, a silk rectangle covered in Japanese writing attached to a long wooden pole. It

flapped in the wind above his head. Around them was a small group of important generals, and men with drums, horns and flags.

"I wish they'd get going," muttered Zuma. "All this waiting is making me nervous."

There was a little bark of agreement from inside her breastplate. Zuma had stored Chilli there to keep him out of harm's way. No one wanted to see a horse accidentally treading on the little dog. Oda was back at the camp, loading up the last salt barrels, and then he was going on to the Dragon's castle to start work in the kitchens.

The Dragon was giving his generals some last-minute orders. Beneath his antlered helmet, he was smiling. It looked like he knew something that no one else did. Climbing up on to his horse, he called Tom and Zuma over.

"The battle will start soon," he told Tom. "My men need to see my banner at all times. Promise me you will never let go of it."

"I promise, Lord Dragon," Tom told him.

He was starting to wish he hadn't been asked to carry the banner. The wooden pole was heavy and his palms were sweaty. He might not have been down at the frontline, but he was still nervous. This wasn't one of his computer games. There were two deadly armies on the plain below him. The danger was very real.

In the distance a horn blasted. The battle had begun.

The Tiger's archers stepped forward and sent a volley of flaming arrows towards the Dragon's men. Then, with a thunderous battle cry, the Tiger's army began rushing across the plain.

"They're coming!" cried Tom.

The Dragon raised his hand. A samurai beside him sounded his horn, and it was the turn of the Dragon's archers to fire arrows at the enemy. Then they too began to charge. The two armies met in the middle of the plain with a deafening crash. Spears tangled and swords clashed. Flaming arrows rained down on both sides.

To Tom, the battle looked like complete mayhem. Beside him the Dragon was silent.

The warlord's eyes flickered in his helmet as he watched the battle. As the warriors fought, Tom realised that the Dragon's men were slowly being forced backwards across the plain.

"We're losing!" said Zuma.

The Dragon turned to her. To Tom's surprise, he grinned.

"Not for long," he said. "Time to try my new strategy." He clapped Tom on the back so hard that Tom nearly dropped the banner. "Move forward so my men can see you," he told him. "Wave the banner high in the air."

Tom took a deep breath. Urging his horse forward, he lifted the silk banner and waved it as hard as he could. Horns were sounding all round him. The Dragon's men cheered in reply.

"Now watch this," said the warlord.

As Tom and Zuma watched, the warriors at the back of the Dragon's army ran forward, replacing the tiring fighters on the frontline. The reinforcements fiercely attacked the Tiger's men.

"You see?" the Dragon told Tom. "If we keep swapping the men at the front of my army, they will stay strong. Soon the Tiger's men will be exhausted."

It didn't take long for the Dragon's strategy to work. Faced with fresh fighters, the Tiger's tired forces started to retreat across the plain. No wonder Oda had called Lord Kenshin a master of warfare.

With his army losing ground, the Tiger himself had to join the battle. He was wearing gleaming golden armour. His headdress looked like a huge mane of white hair. The Tiger spurred his horse into the thick of the fighting, cutting a path through the Dragon's men.

"Truly, Lord Shingen is a worthy rival," said the Dragon. "Tom, signal my front and back lines to swap places again."

But this time, when Tom rode forward, the Tiger pointed his sword straight at him.

"Listen up, men!" he yelled to his troops.

"Stop that boy sending signals! Capture that banner!"

The Tiger's men roared back, and immediately began fighting their way towards Tom and Zuma's hill.

"Uh-oh!" said Zuma. "This doesn't look good." Chilli whimpered, and buried himself deeper behind her breastplate.

"Aha! Perhaps we will fight after all," said the Dragon. He sounded quite happy about the idea.

Tom swallowed nervously. It felt like the Tiger's whole army was after him now. He forced himself to stand firm. He had promised the Dragon he wouldn't drop the banner.

The Tiger was swinging his sword as he led a group of samurai up the hillside towards Tom and Zuma.

"Stand back," the Dragon ordered,

drawing his sword. "Leave the Tiger to me!"

The two warlords met with a loud clash of steel. The Tiger swung his sword, only to be blocked by the Dragon's blade. Then they circled each other, waiting for the best moment to strike.

"Look out, Tom!" Zuma shouted.

Twisting in the saddle, Tom saw an enemy warrior galloping towards him. Tom had a sword strapped to his belt, but he'd have to drop the banner if he wanted to use it. Then he remembered – during his adventures with Princess Isis, he had seen knights jousting on horseback. He didn't have a lance, but he did have a banner...

The samurai stood up in his saddle and raised his sword. As the man galloped nearer, Tom lowered his banner pole until it was pointing straight at him. The samurai tried to stop his horse, but he was travelling too quickly. The tip of the banner struck him squarely in the chest, sending him flying from his saddle!

"Well done, Tom!" roared the Dragon.

The rest of the army let out a loud cheer as Tom raised the banner high into the air. The Tiger chose that moment to charge at the Dragon. Pulling back his arm, the Dragon hurled a dagger at the Tiger. Quick as a flash, the Tiger pulled something small and metal from inside his armour. He opened it with a flick of his wrist to make a fan.

Tom remembered seeing a similar weapon in his dad's museum. It was a Japanese

war fan called a *tessen*. Only this fan was different to the one in the museum display. Its handle was inlaid with a gold coin with a picture of a sun on it – Tlaloc's coin!

Tom gasped as the Tiger swung his war fan through the air. With a *clang*, the Dragon's dagger was knocked aside. It spun away into the grass.

Before the Tiger could charge at the Dragon again, a shout from Zuma stopped him in his tracks.

"Look!" she cried. "The Tiger's army is running away!"

Cursing, the Tiger looked round. What remained of his army was stumbling away from the battlefield. He wheeled his horse off and galloped down the hill after his men. "Until next time, Lord Dragon!" he called over his shoulder.

"Did you see that?" Zuma asked Tom. "Tlaloc's coin! The Tiger has it in his fan!"

Tom's reply was drowned out by the sound of a roaring Dragon.

"Victory!" bellowed Lord Kenshin, raising his sword into the air. "Victory is ours!"

His army answered with a rumbling cheer.

CHAPTER 7
DON'T LOOK DOWN

"What are we going to do?" Zuma moaned.
"We're travelling with the wrong army!"

For once, Tom wasn't sure what to say.
The Dragon's camp had been packed up,
and his army was on its way back to the
castle. After Tom's heroics with the banner,
he and Zuma had been made guests of
honour at a victory feast that night. Although
Tom was relieved he and Zuma had come
through the battle unhurt, every mile was

taking them further away from Tlaloc's coin.
And without it, neither of them would ever
see home again!

"Maybe we should have tried to grab
the fan while the Tiger was fighting the
Dragon," Zuma said thoughtfully.

"You've got to be joking!" said Tom.
"Anyway, Lord Kenshin told his men that he
would fight the Tiger alone. It would have
been dishonourable to disobey him."

Zuma rolled her eyes. "Honour this and
honour that," she said. "If you spend any
more time with these samurai, you'll soon be
bowing at the ants. Honestly, I—" She broke
off.

"What's the matter?" Tom asked.

Zuma said nothing. She was staring
straight ahead. They had left the grassy plain
behind and followed a narrow path through

the hills. Now they had come to the edge of a deep gorge. The only way across the steep drop was a narrow bridge made of wooden planks lashed together with rope.

"I am NOT crossing that," said Zuma, folding her arms. "No way."

"We have to," Tom replied. "Everyone else is."

"I don't care."

"It's only a bridge," said Tom. "What's the problem?"

Zuma's face turned red. "I don't like heights," she mumbled.

Tom laughed out loud. "It'll be fine," he told her. "Come on, I'll help you."

But as they neared the bridge, Tom felt his confidence fading. It really was a very long way down. And at the bottom of the gorge, a rushing river of water swirled round sharp, jagged rocks. Up close, the bridge looked even more rickety. It swayed in the breeze and creaked as the warriors led their horses over it.

Zuma insisted on waiting right until the end before crossing. The last of the Dragon's army had disappeared down the path by the time Tom and Zuma set their horses on the bridge. If they didn't get a move on, they'd be left behind.

"Let's go," said Tom. "And whatever you do, don't look down."

Gripping the ropes and clenching her teeth, Zuma put a foot on to the bridge. As if to show her it was safe, Chilli jumped out of her breastplate and scampered across the planks to the other side of the gorge. He barked happily.

"See?" said Tom, laughing. "Even Chilli says it's OK."

Zuma said nothing. Slowly they made their way along, moving one step at a time from one plank to another. It seemed to take an age just to get halfway across. Zuma wasn't in any mood to rush, though.

Suddenly, the sky darkened, and there was a loud rumble of thunder.

"Oh no!" Zuma groaned. "Not now!"

Huge grey clouds formed into a familiar face with bulging eyes and sharp fangs. Tlaloc's laughter echoed round the gorge.

"Did you think I would make it easy for you?" boomed the rain god. "Let's see how you get on now!"

A strong gust of wind attacked the bridge, making it wobble and shake. Rain poured down on Tom and Zuma, soaking their clothes. All they could do was cling desperately on to the ropes and pray for the storm to end.

"Stop it, Tlaloc!" shouted Zuma. "You'll blow us off the bridge!"

The rain god cackled with laughter. Tom could hear the bridge creaking loudly over the noise of the storm. *How long before the ropes snap?* he wondered. He looked down at the jagged rocks below and gulped.

"We've got to get out of here!" he shouted to Zuma.

Zuma nodded, gritting her teeth. The rain had made the wooden planks slippery, making their journey even more treacherous. Desperate not to look down, Tom fixed his eyes on Chilli at the other side of the gorge. The little Chihuahua was beside himself, bouncing up and down and barking wildly.

They were only a few steps from safety when the storm grew worse, and the wind howled more loudly than ever. A rope

snapped with a loud *twang*, and the bridge
twisted and sagged. Tom tumbled over the
guide rope and found himself staring down at
the bottom of the gorge. His stomach did a
somersault.

Then a hand grabbed his arm, and Zuma
pulled him back up. "The bridge won't hold
much longer!" she yelled.

Together they raced across the final few planks and on to solid ground just in time. A second later the bridge fell away with a final groan, plunging into the raging water below.

Tom and Zuma collapsed, too exhausted to speak. For a second Tom thought it was raining harder than ever, and then he realised it was only Chilli licking his face. The clouds had gone. Tlaloc's storm had passed.

"That was close," Tom panted. "Thanks for saving me back there."

"What happened to 'Don't look down.'?" asked Zuma.

"I forgot."

Zuma stared at him, and then they both started laughing.

Once they had found their horses and got back in the saddle, Tom and Zuma soon managed to catch up with the rest of the army. The Dragon had stopped, and was talking to a ragged group of men at the side of the road. As Tom and Zuma rode up, one of the men stepped forward and gave a low bow.

"Oh, famous and mighty Lord Dragon," he said in a deep voice. "I am Hideo, the leader of these hungry musicians. We heard news of your triumph and wondered if such a noble lord would allow wretches like us to play at his victory feast?" The man lifted a flute to his lips and played a little tune.

The Dragon nodded. "My castle is not far. You shall have shelter and food. Tonight I will listen to your music."

Hideo bowed again. "My Lord Dragon is as generous as he is powerful," he said.

The Dragon spurred his horse forward. Hideo and his men followed on foot. Tom and Zuma were soon riding in the middle of them.

To Tom's surprise, Hideo recognised him. "Ah," he said. "You must be the boy who carried the Dragon's banner."

Puzzled, Tom stared at him.

Hideo laughed at the look on Tom's face. "News travels fast," he explained. "They say you brought luck to the Lord Dragon."

Tom smiled. "All I did was sit on a horse and hold a flag," he said.

"A mighty deed. I shall write a song about it." As Tom laughed, Hideo kicked his heels in the air and played another little tune on his flute.

"Look, Tom," Zuma interrupted. Her voice sounded excited.

Tom lifted his head. The Dragon's castle stood on a hill, surrounded by high walls.

At the top was a tall tower. Round it were buildings with white walls and grey, sloping roofs that turned upwards at the corners.

"What a strange-looking castle," said Zuma, pointing at the tower. "It looks more like a load of houses built on top of each other."

"I think it's called a pagoda," Tom said. He urged his horse forward. "Come on. Oda will already be in the kitchens. Let's go and find him."

"Good idea," said Zuma. "Chilli is starving. As usual."

Oda gave them a beaming smile when he saw them.

"My friends," he said. "You made it through the battle!"

Zuma rushed over and hugged the tall

teenager. Tom followed just in time to hear her say, "You're cutting those onions all wrong, you know. When I was a slave I had to chop vegetables all the time. Here, let me show you." Grabbing the knife from Oda's hand, she began slicing at top speed.

Grinning, Tom said, "Have you made a lot of food?"

"Enough for three victory feasts," Oda said proudly. "Cooking isn't as interesting as fighting, though. Tell me *everything*."

Tom told him about their adventures until a loud chiming sound rang out.

Zuma jumped up. "Tlaloc!" she squeaked.

Oda looked confused. "It's just the gong telling everyone the feast is about to start," he said. "You'd better hurry."

Tom and Zuma ran. At the doors of the castle's feasting hall two guards bowed them

through. Inside, men in colourful kimonos
and women with white-painted faces and
fancy hairstyles sat at long tables.

"Ah! My banner carrier and his brave companion," boomed the Dragon, spotting them. He stood and held up his cup. "Thanks to them, we were able to clip the mighty Tiger's claws. Come, sit at my table. Tonight we celebrate a great victory—"

He was interrupted by one of the guards. "My Lord, a messenger has arrived from the Tiger!"

"Bring him in at once," the Dragon barked.

A samurai was led in. "Lord Kenshin," he said with a bow. "Lord Shingen congratulates you on a battle fought with skill and honour. He sends this gift to mark your victory."

Tom and Zuma gasped. The messenger was holding out the Tiger's war fan, with Tlaloc's gold coin glittering in the handle!

CHAPTER 8
BUMP IN THE NIGHT

Outside the Dragon's castle, the sky was growing dark. Inside the feasting hall, servants lit paper lanterns, casting a merry glow over the guests. A constant stream of delicious food arrived at Tom and Zuma's table. All round them, samurai swapped stories about the battle. But Tom and Zuma weren't listening. They just kept staring at the war fan that lay on the table in front of the Dragon.

"We could just snatch it and run for it," Zuma whispered.

"Don't you remember the riddle?" said Tom. "It said 'Heroes not thieves will get their reward.'"

"So?" replied Zuma. "We're not thieves."

"If we try and steal the war fan we will be."

Zuma sighed. Putting her elbows on the table, she rested her chin in her hands and gazed at the fan. "We're *soooo* close," she groaned.

"Just be patient," Tom told her. "We'll get Tlaloc's coin somehow."

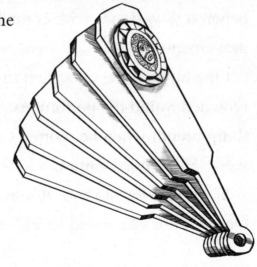

Eventually the warriors finished eating and servants began clearing the feast away. At the end of the hall, Hideo entered with his band of musicians. They had changed into red and white kimonos and decorated headdresses. They sat down on rugs and arranged their instruments. Tom saw different kinds of drums as well as a stringed instrument that looked a little like a guitar. At Hideo's nod, the band began to play. A woman wearing a trailing robe stepped forward and began a slow dance with complicated hand movements.

One by one, the guests left their tables and crowded round the performers. Tom took a sharp breath when he spotted Goro among them. He nudged Zuma.

She had seen him too. A scowl crossed her face. "What's he doing here?" she said. "I thought he was in disgrace."

"Lord Kenshin must have forgiven him,"
Tom replied.

Goro was sniggering and joking with a
group of his friends, not bothering to watch
the musicians play. When he saw Oda enter
the feasting hall to help
clear away the food, he
nudged his friends.
Goro waited for
Oda to walk past
him carrying
a large bowl
of rice, then
stuck out a leg,
tripping him up.
Oda stumbled,
spilling rice all
over the floor.

Goro's friends roared with laughter.

"What a clumsy oaf!" crowed Goro.

The Dragon looked over, his eyes narrowing. Goro hastily put on an innocent expression.

"Here, I'll help!" he said loudly. He kneeled down beside the red-faced Oda and helped scoop the spilled rice back into the bowl.

"What a snake!" said Zuma. "Goro was the one who tripped him up, and now he's pretending to help him!"

Goro patted Oda on the back. "All cleaned up," he said, loud enough for the Dragon to hear. "No need to thank me."

Oda's face was burning with embarrassment. He bowed quickly and hurried out of the feasting hall. When the Dragon turned back to the musicians, Goro looked across at Tom and gave him a nasty smirk.

"He hasn't changed," said Tom.

"Oda should challenge him to a wrestling match," said Zuma. "That would wipe the smile off Goro's face."

"I don't think he can," Tom replied. "Goro may be a sneak, but he's a nobleman's son. Oda's just an ordinary villager. He can't go round picking fights with people like Goro."

A crescent moon was high in the sky by the time the musicians finished playing and the guests began to leave. "Shall we go to bed?" Tom yawned.

Looking longingly at the war fan, Zuma sighed. "I suppose so," she replied. She followed Tom to the room they had been given. It was clean and simple. Two low beds stood at opposite ends. Between them a window looked down on to a courtyard garden where a single lantern glowed.

Tom climbed into bed gratefully. It felt like a long time since he had last rested. He pulled the sheet up to his chin, and within seconds he was asleep.

A growl woke him up. Tom opened one eye. The moon was lower in the sky, but it was still the middle of the night. Chilli was standing by his head. The little Chihuahua was looking down through the window at the garden below, growling softly.

"Shh," Tom said, pushing him away. Chilli carried on growling. "Take him out for a walk, Zuma," he groaned.

Zuma sat up, rubbing her eyes. Chilli was still staring at the window, the short fur on the back of his neck standing on end.

"He doesn't look like he wants a walk,"
said Zuma. "I think he's trying to warn us
about something."

Tom sighed and climbed out of bed. "Then
we'd better go down and see what the

problem is," he said.

As soon as Tom opened the bedroom door, Chilli ran through it like a rocket. At the top of the stairs, the little dog stopped and looked back. It was clear he wanted Tom and Zuma to follow him. Together, they silently followed the little dog. Soon, the three of them stood by an open door that led into the garden.

Tom peered out. Through the dim light of the lantern, he could make out small, neat trees and wooden benches. A gravel path wound past a small pond with a trickling waterfall. The garden was as still and silent as a grave.

"False alarm," Tom whispered to Zuma. "There's no one—"

He stopped talking as a figure dressed in black stepped out from the shadows by the far wall. As Tom watched, the man reached into the lantern and snuffed out the candle. The garden was plunged into blackness.

"What happened?" hissed Zuma. "Who's there?"

Tom turned and looked at her, his eyes wide. "It's a ninja," he whispered. "There's an assassin on the loose!"

CHAPTER 9
INSTRUMENT OF DEATH

The ninja darted away through the darkness. Tom and Zuma followed as quietly as they could. Chilli prowled beside them like a wolf stalking its prey. Moving through the shadows, the ninja walked quickly and silently along the path.

Snap.

Tom had stepped on a twig. In the quiet of the garden, it sounded like a gun had gone off. Instantly, the ninja stopped and dropped into a crouch. One hand reached over his shoulder and clutched the hilt of his sword.

Zuma grabbed Tom by the arm and pulled him behind a tree. A second later, the ninja turned his head and stared in their direction. The assassin didn't move. Neither did Tom, Zuma or Chilli. Tom held his breath, certain that his pounding heartbeat would give them away.

The ninja was as still as a rock, searching for any sign that he had been seen. Then, after what seemed like hours, he stood up. With a final glance round, he carried on along the path.

Tom let out his breath in a slow hiss. Turning to Zuma, he mouthed the word 'Sorry'. She grinned, and they started to follow the ninja again. This time, Tom was extra careful where he put his feet.

A few moments later, Zuma stopped and pointed ahead. The ninja was at the foot of the castle wall, gazing up at an open window.

Tom's eyes widened. Leaning close to Zuma, he whispered into her ear. "He's right under the Dragon's room. Oda told me it's the highest room in the tower."

The ninja unwound a rope from round his waist. At one end was a piece of metal with four hooks. He swung it expertly and let go. The hook flew into the air and, with a soft *clunk*, it caught on the windowsill. The ninja tested the rope. It held firm. He began to climb up the wall like a deadly spider.

Zuma had already turned away and was heading back the way they had came.

"Where are you going?" hissed Tom.

"Where do you think?" she said. "We have to warn the Dragon!"

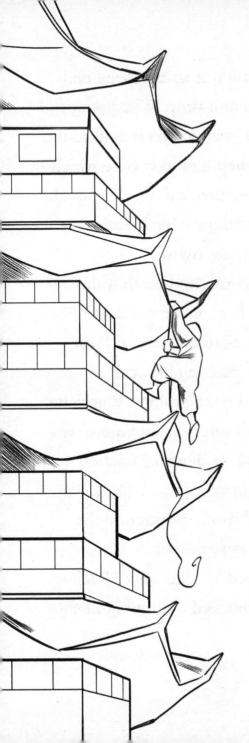

She raced
off through
the garden,
and Tom had
to work hard
to keep up.
He knew they
were in a race
against time. A
ruthless killer
was climbing
up towards the
Dragon's room.
Lord Kenshin's
life was hanging
by a thread.

Together
Tom, Zuma and
Chilli sprinted

back to the castle and ran up the staircase, taking the steps two at a time. When they reached the top, the corridor veered off to the left and the right. They had to choose which way to go – and they didn't have time to make a mistake. Taking a deep breath, Tom went left, hoping he was right.

They rounded a corner to find that the corridor ended at a heavily carved door. With a deep breath Tom and Zuma burst through it together, crashing into the Dragon's bedroom. Lord Kenshin sat upright in bed, grunting with surprise. The ninja was standing by the window. He was holding a wooden pipe to his lips.

"Look out!" cried Tom, pointing to the ninja. "He's got a blowpipe!"

The Dragon moved like lightning. Rolling over in his bed, he reached out and grabbed

the war fan from beside his bed. With a flick
of his wrist, it opened. The ninja blew into
his pipe, and there was a *clink* as the Dragon
batted the poisoned dart out of the air.

Cursing, the ninja sprang into the room. He reached over his shoulder and grasped the hilt of his sword. The Dragon was unarmed except for the metal fan. Tom and Zuma had to protect him!

Tom reached into his pocket and grasped the only weapon he had – the pouch of salt that Oda had given him. He pulled out the bag and threw its contents at the assassin's face. The ninja screamed as the salt stung his eyes. Blinded, he crashed into a table.

"Here, Dragon!" shouted Zuma. "Catch!" She had picked up a sword from the weapons rack on the wall, and threw it to the warlord. Leaping from his bed, the Dragon caught it in mid-air. A second later, the ninja was pinned to the wall, a razor-sharp blade at his throat. With his spare hand, the Dragon ripped off the ninja's black hood. Tom and

Zuma instantly recognised the assassin's angry face.

"Hideo!" Tom gasped. "The musician."

He looked down to see that Hideo was still holding his flute in his hand. All along, his musical instrument had been a blowpipe in disguise!

"Who sent you?" the Dragon demanded. His voice was a menacing growl.

Hideo scowled. "You will never know," he replied. "A ninja never tells who has hired him."

"The Tiger!" Zuma said. "It *has* to be the Tiger."

Without taking his eyes off Hideo, the Dragon said, "No. The Tiger would kill me in battle. He would never hire a vile ninja to murder me in my sleep."

Something glinted on Hideo's finger. With

a frown, Tom leaned forward. Hideo was wearing a ring that Tom was sure he recognised. His eyes widened when he remembered. "I know who hired him!" he gasped.

"Impossible," Hideo snarled.

"Not impossible," Tom replied. He pointed at Hideo's finger. "Last time I saw that ring it was on Goro's finger. He must have given it to you as payment when he hired you."

"Goro!" the Dragon snapped. "He will die for this... no, he will be banished to wander as a beggar for the rest of his life. The shame will be worse than death."

The sound of fighting in the Dragon's room had woken up the whole castle. Guards were rushing in. "Take him," the Dragon ordered, shoving Hideo towards them. "Throw him in jail. Be careful, ninjas always carry hidden weapons. And send men to arrest Goro."

As the guards dragged Hideo away, the Dragon turned to Tom and Zuma. To their surprise, the mighty warlord gave them a deep bow. "I owe you my life," he told Tom. "Name your reward. Would you like to become a samurai in my army? Your courage would be welcome among us."

"I'd love to, Lord Dragon," said Tom. "But we have to leave soon."

"A shame," said the warlord. "I needed a new water taster. The last one was poisoned." He roared with laughter, and gave Tom a hearty clap on the back. "I am joking. Your courage will be missed, though."

Tom had a thought. "There is a boy in your kitchens who would love to join the samurai, though. His name is Oda."

"The salt thief? I remember him," said the Dragon, frowning.

"He's very strong," said Zuma. "And he beat a champion wrestler called Kashegi."

The Dragon looked impressed. "Really? That's a match I would like to have seen."

"He's also brave and loyal," Tom added. "Oda would make an excellent samurai."

The Dragon clapped his hands together. "It shall be done. First thing in the morning I will speak to your friend. He will begin his training immediately."

Tom and Zuma grinned at each other. They knew how happy Oda would be to hear the news. And the Dragon hadn't finished yet.

"If you cannot join my army, please

accept this gift," he said, handing an object
to Tom. "As a thank-you for saving my
life."

It was the war fan with Tlaloc's coin in the
handle!

"This helped protect me," the Dragon said, smiling. "Perhaps it will be good for you too."

Tom didn't know what to say. He bowed. Chilli barked with delight.

When Zuma reached out and touched the war fan, thunder rumbled in the distance and a mist appeared.

"Here we go again," said Zuma.

Tom just had time to call out, "Thank you, Lord Dragon," before the mist wrapped them up in a whirlwind and pulled them back through time.

CHAPTER 10
GAME ON

Tom felt soft carpet beneath his feet. A
second later, Chilli dropped out of nowhere.
Tom caught the little dog before he hit the
floor. Chilli thanked him with a faceful of
licks. Zuma was last to appear.

"That was *so* weird," she laughed as the
remains of the mist disappeared. "But fun.
It's definitely the best bit about time travel."
Her kimono had gone. Once again, she was
wearing her feathered headdress and her

face was painted blue. The black pendant gleamed at her throat.

Tom had to agree. He was pleased to be back in his own bedroom, though. Time travel was exciting, but it was good to be home. He looked round his room at the crowded bookcases and his computer and the mess of comics on the floor. Everything was just as he had left it. While they were away, time had stood still in his own world.

"We did it, Tom!" Zuma cheered, waving the Tiger's fan. She jumped about in an Aztec victory dance. "That's two coins now!"

"I think it's time I taught you how to high-five," Tom said. He held up one hand. A grin spread across his face as Zuma slapped his palm. Once again they had survived Tlaloc's quest. And no matter how scary and dangerous their adventures were, it would

be worth it if Zuma won back her life and
freedom. *Plus, I get to visit some brilliant places,*
Tom thought. Medieval Japan had been
amazing.

"Next time I'm not walking over any bridges, though," Zuma said firmly. "Not for all the gold coins in Tlaloc's frilly purse."

"Shh!" Tom warned. "If he hears you, he'll

put bridges in every quest from now on!"

As if Tlaloc had been listening, a rumble of thunder echoed round the room. Tom, Zuma and Chilli looked up at the ceiling. Rain spattered down on their faces. Above, clouds swirled until they formed the goggle-eyed shape of the rain god's face.

"So, you have passed my second test," Tlaloc growled. His feathered headdress shook with anger. "But you have not won yet. Four coins remain and I promise you, you won't be so lucky next time."

"Don't count on it," Zuma said boldly. "Tom and I make a pretty good team."

"Whatever you throw at us, we'll find those coins, Tlaloc," Tom added.

Tlaloc scowled. "Give me the coin," he demanded. Zuma dropped the fan into his hand. Tlaloc's fingers closed round it.

"You will not need to wait long for your next quest," he said. "So prepare yourselves… it will be deadly." Then with a final snarl, Tlaloc vanished.

The rain stopped and the clouds disappeared. At the same moment, Tom's bedroom door opened. His mum peered in. "Did I hear you talking to yourself, Tom?" she asked.

"Um… yeah," Tom replied. He tried not to look at Zuma, who was invisible to his mum. It didn't help that Zuma was holding her sides, laughing.

"It's the first sign of madness, you know," said his mum.

"Well, there was no one *sensible* to talk to," Tom replied, with a sideways glance at the Aztec girl.

Zuma poked out her tongue at him.

"You spend too much time indoors," said his mum. "The rain has cleared up. Why don't you go outside?" She smiled and headed back out of the room.

If only she knew where I'd just been! Tom thought to himself.

Out of the window Tom could see it was a sunny day again. Perfect tennis weather. "Come on," he told Zuma. "Time for a game of tennis. Race you outside."

"Hey, wait for me!" With Chilli yapping excitedly at her heels, Zuma snatched up the racquet and ran after Tom. "And don't forget your weapon!" she yelled.

WHO WERE THE MIGHTIEST SAMURAI?

Lord Kenshin was a *real* warlord! Find out more about him and other famous Samurai.

LORD UESUGI KENSHIN was one of the most powerful and respected daimyo (warlords) in 16th-century Japan, famous for his many battles against his rival Lord Shingen. Their armies fought five times in the same place, Kawanakajima. When he heard of Lord Shingen's death, Lord Kenshin was so sad he cried and ordered that no music be played in his castle for three days.

LORD TAKEDA SHINGEN may have dressed like a monk and written poetry as a child, but he was one of the fiercest daimyo around. He punished criminals by boiling them alive in two giant iron cauldrons! In 1565 Lord Shingen foiled an assassination plot against him led by his own son, Yoshinobu. He punished Yoshinobu by confining him to a temple for two years. Grounded! Lord Shingen died in 1573 whilst laying siege to a castle with his army. Many people believe he was shot by a sniper who was hiding up on the castle walls.

HATTORI HANZO was both a samurai and a ninja. He fought in his first battle when he was just sixteen years old, his fighting skills earning him the nickname 'Devil Hanzo'. In 1582 Hattori helped a daimyo called Tokugawa Ieyasu escape from the territory of an enemy lord. When Ieyasu later became shogun, the most powerful man in Japan, Hattori became his loyal servant, leading a 200-man unit of ninjas from the Iga clan who acted as spies, guards and assassins for the shogun. Many people believed that Hattori had supernatural powers, including the ability to vanish and reappear whenever he wanted!

HONDA TADAKATSU was a samurai general who served under the shogun Tokugawa Ieyasu. He was such a skilled warrior that he was said never to have been wounded – despite taking part in over 100 battles! He once challenged an army to fight even though he was outnumbered 50 to 1. The opposing general was so impressed by Honda's bravery he ordered his men not to attack him. Honda carried a spear that was known as 'Dragonfly Cutter', because it was so sharp that an insect once landed on it and was sliced in half. Now that's a lethal weapon!